To Yüksel
With Best wishes.
from

Sandra Lightburn.

November 1999

DRIFTWOOD
COVE

WRITTEN BY SANDRA LIGHTBURN

ILLUSTRATED BY RON LIGHTBURN

DOUBLEDAY CANADA LIMITED

"Race you to Shack Island!" called Matthew to his sister Katelyn.

"Have you checked the tide chart?" asked their grandfather. "You don't want to be marooned on that big rock. When the tide comes in it's a long swim back to shore."

"The chart shows it won't be high tide until three o'clock," answered Matthew as he munched on a piece of toast.

"Are you coming with us, Grandma?" Katelyn added. "Maybe we'll meet up with the ghost Grandpa saw when you were camping here last summer."

"I didn't say anything about a ghost," their grandfather chuckled. "It was a foggy day, and through the mist I thought I saw a girl poking around that old shack on the island. When the fog cleared, I wandered over to investigate but didn't find anyone."

"She didn't come past our camp spot, and this is the only path from the beach to the road," explained their grandmother. "We don't know who built that shack, but it's been empty for many years." She turned to their grandfather. "Are you sure it was a girl? Maybe you saw a heron, or a big seagull."

"I know what I saw," he said, as he slowly cleaned his glasses with his handkerchief.

"You kids go on down to the beach," laughed their grandmother. She handed them some sandwiches in a bag. "Your grandfather and I will wash the breakfast dishes — you enjoy your holiday on the coast. And don't talk to any strangers, especially if they're ghosts," she said with a wink.

Following the overgrown path, Matthew and Katelyn wound their way down to the beach. The ancient rain forest smelled of damp and decay. Leaving the gloomy forest behind, the path led them to the shore warmed by the morning sun. As they ran out to the island, their footprint trails quickly disappeared in the soft, wet sand.

"I win!" shouted Matthew when he reached the island two steps ahead of Katelyn.

They scrambled along the rocks, over the smooth carpet of moss and up to the shack.

Katelyn slowly opened the paint-peeled door. Inside the old building sat a wobbly table and chair. The dusty floor was covered with wood shavings. Pictures of animals had been carved into the wooden walls.

As Matthew moved closer to study the simple shapes of seagulls, squirrels, and deer, he stumbled over a gap in the floor.

"Hey! This board is loose." He removed the rotting plank, home to several shiny black beetles.

Katelyn peered into the dark space under the floor and saw a twinkling of colour.

"There's something down there."

Matthew lifted out a lumpy brown basket of woven kelp and carefully emptied some of its contents onto the table.

Out spilled a rainbow of shiny abalone shells, pink spiky sea urchins, fragile sand dollars, and jewel-coloured beach glass that the endless washing of waves had rounded and dulled. Some pieces had been strung together to form pendants.

"Is this the ghost's treasure?" asked Matthew.

"What would a ghost want with treasure?" laughed Katelyn, as she picked out a pendant of a delicately carved wooden goat on a thin leather thong. The miniature animal was cedar brown, with what looked like a tiny bell around its neck. "But if it's not the ghost's treasure, who does it belong to?" Katelyn wondered, as she slipped the pendant over her head.

The mysterious owner was soon forgotten as they sorted through the colourful pile. During the next few hours they made up stories about their favourite pieces. The crab shell, a thorny shield for a lilliputian warrior; the oyster shell, rough with craters like the surface of the moon; the key that could open a bulging sunken treasure chest; the limpet shells that looked like miniature snow-capped mountains; the worn old coins lost by Spanish explorers; and the mussel shell, a tiny sea monster with barnacle eyes.

Katelyn nibbled on a salmon sandwich and imagined that the decrepit shack had changed into a cosy cottage by the sea. "I wish we could always live here," she sighed dreamily.

As she slowly drifted out of her fantasy, she became aware of cold fingers of fog on her neck and down her back. Shivering from the damp chill, she glanced outside.

"It's gone," she whispered.

"What's gone?" asked Matthew, looking up from the table.

"The beach — everything!"

Matthew stared out the window. He couldn't see anything beyond the shack but a heavy blanket of fog.

"The whole world has disappeared." He checked his watch. "It's almost two o'clock! The tide must be coming in!"

They inched their way off the island, then hesitated. The thick grey mist billowed and rolled, curled back upon itself and hid the world from them.

"How are we supposed to find the path when we can't even see the trees?" asked Matthew.

Katelyn held her little brother's hand. "I'm sure it's this way," she said, as they stumbled along in the dense fog. Their shoes slapped in the shallow tidal water that had crept over the sand.

A strange sound from somewhere ahead broke the long silence. They stopped and listened.

"That's no seagull." Katelyn held her breath, and Matthew started to tremble.

"What if it's a … a cougar or a bear, or … or the ghost!" he stammered. "Where can we hide?" They stood like statues and strained to see what was lurking in the dank fog.

Suddenly, a scruffy-looking creature appeared before them. It gazed at the disbelieving pair and shook its head. Clank went the bell around its neck.

"A goat! How did a goat get here?"

Katelyn calmed the nervous animal with a soothing rub behind its ears. "Who do you belong to?"

"Me," said a haunting voice, and a ghostly figure emerged from a swirl of mist. Katelyn and Matthew drew back as a barefoot girl slowly approached the goat. "It's a good thing you wear that bell," she gently scolded, "or I'd never find you." Then she turned and gave Katelyn a curious stare. "You're wearing my pendant."

Katelyn blushed. In their haste to get off the island she had forgotten all about the pendant. She fumbled with it as she took it off.

"I didn't know it was yours," she mumbled, sheepishly handing the pendant to the girl. There was an awkward moment of silence. "I'm Katelyn and this is my brother Matthew. We got lost in the fog trying to find the path to our camp spot," she explained. "We had to get off Shack Island in a hurry because the tide was coming in, but we didn't know which way to go."

The girl continued to stare at them, then grabbed the goat by its collar. "My name is Salena. Come on. I can help you."

Hesitantly, they followed Salena and her goat down the long, hazy beach. Far ahead they saw the faint outline of a large, unfamiliar shape. As they walked closer, they could see what looked like a rambling tree house on the ground.

A woman with a concerned expression appeared at the door. "You three must be chilled to the bone after wandering around in this damp fog."

Matthew looked at his sister. "Grandma told us not to talk to strangers," he warned, "or ghosts."

"They're not ghosts," Katelyn whispered back.

"This is Katelyn," Salena said, "and her brother Matthew."

"I'm Mary and this is Rob," the woman explained, as a tall man with a toothy grin joined her. "Let me get you wrapped up in warm blankets by the fire, and I'll make a drink of hot milk for everyone."

The children were soon snuggled by the warm wood stove, bundled in soft blankets that smelled of the sea. Katelyn sipped from her steaming mug and looked around the room. Some of the larger windows had plastic sheeting instead of glass. Propane lamps cast haloes of golden light onto the rugged wooden walls. There was no TV.

"Is this your summer cottage?" Katelyn asked.

"No, we live here all the time," replied Salena.

Mary smiled softly and looked at Rob. "We came to Driftwood Cove to camp and never left. It seemed like home to us."

"Mom and Dad built our house in these huge, hollow trees, using scrap lumber and logs that the tide washed up on the beach," added Salena. "We use the best pieces of driftwood for carvings, then sell them at the market in town."

"Do you buy your food in town?" asked Matthew.

"Not very much," replied Rob. "We catch plenty of fish, and what we don't need we sell at the market. If the fish aren't biting, the crab traps are usually full. We also have a big vegetable garden, and in the forest we pick mushrooms and berries. There's always something we can put together for a good meal. Fresh water comes from a stream behind the house, and we get our milk from Elsie."

"Elsie's our goat," Salena explained.

Matthew swallowed as he looked uneasily into his nearly empty mug.

"We're lucky because the person who owns this land doesn't mind us living here," added Mary. "Squatters aren't always welcome."

"Is your last name Squatter?" asked Matthew.

Salena giggled, and her mom and dad laughed. "No," answered Mary. "We're called squatters because we don't own or rent the land."

"But if you live here all year long, where does Salena go to school?"

"Salena gets home schooling." Mary pointed to shelves that were bent under the weight of stacks of books. "We also take turns reading to each other every day."

"And my dad teaches me how to carve," Salena added proudly. "I made this pendant."

"Maybe Katelyn and Matthew would like to learn how to carve, too." Rob picked up a piece of driftwood and turned it over in his hands. "I've been waiting for this wood to tell me what it wants to be," he said. "I hold it and study it. Then I hear it softly whisper to me. This piece of driftwood just told me it wants to be a whale. You see here, where the knot in the wood is a different colour? Well, that's just like the different colours on a killer whale."

"Can *anyone* hear the wood whisper?" asked Matthew excitedly.

"Sure, but first you have to know how to carve. Watch while I work on this piece. I draw the guidelines first, then I start to cut."

Matthew and Katelyn tried to memorize every movement of Rob's large, steady hands while he slowly peeled away the wood. Bit by bit and layer by layer, the rounded shape of a killer whale emerged. As Rob worked, the room filled with the sharp scent of raw cedar, while the pile of curled wood shavings grew on the floor by his feet.

"Finally, that fog has lifted." Dust motes sparkled in a swirling dance, surrounding Mary like pixie dust as she stood in a warm beam of sunshine.

Rob squinted out the window to check the tide level. "Salena and I had better take you two back to your path by boat. The tide is in and you won't be able to walk along the beach to get there."

As the boat neared the shore, Katelyn and Matthew spied their grandparents anxiously searching for them.

"Grandpa! Grandma! Here we are!" they yelled.

Their grandparents looked up in surprise and relief to see the two children scramble out of a small, unsteady boat.

Rob introduced himself and explained that the kids had spent the afternoon at his family's house on the beach. "Now that the weather has cleared," he said, "we might catch some fish on the way home. Why don't you all come down and have dinner with us tonight? The tide will be going out again by then. Just follow the beach around the point, past the uprooted tree, and you'll find us."

"It's okay, Grandma," said Matthew. "They're not strangers any more."

That evening Katelyn, Matthew, and their grandparents each brought a contribution to the dinner. Matthew made sure that he took lots of marshmallows for roasting over the fire.

"Welcome to Driftwood Cove!" called Mary, as she waved them towards the food-laden table. "The fish were biting, so we're having a salmon barbecue tonight. But first there's a bucket of fresh crab to gobble down!"

After a huge meal, they lingered around the faint glow of the dying fire. Salena removed the goat pendant and gave it a long, thoughtful look.

"I want you to keep it," she smiled, as she placed the pendant in Katelyn's hand. "It will remind you to come see me again."

Katelyn gazed down at the treasured gift from her new friend. "Do you ever get lonely here?"

"Sometimes friends of my mom and dad come to live on the beach for a while," said Salena quietly. She looked over at Matthew, who was gathering driftwood. "And Mom says I'm going to have lots of brothers and sisters."

"You can have Matthew if you want," smiled Katelyn. They both giggled.

Matthew staggered under the weight of an enormous armload of wood. "I'm taking this home with me so I can listen to it whisper," he told Salena. "Then when we come back next summer, I'll bring you my best carving. You'll still be here, won't you?"

"Sure," replied Salena. "This is my home."

For Mom and Dad — wish you were here to share my books and stroll through my garden.
With sincere appreciation to John, Maggie and Don for having faith.
S.L.

For all those who call the West Coast home.
With thanks to the Baxter, Symons and Thompson families for your patience and friendship.
R.L.

Copyright ©1998 Sandra Lightburn (text), Ron Lightburn (illustrations)

Canadian Cataloguing in Publication Data

Lightburn, Sandra
Driftwood Cove

ISBN 0-385-25626-4

I. Lightburn, Ron. II. Title.

PS8573.I415D74 1998   jC813'.54   C98-931756-0
PZ7.L53Dr 1998

The illustrations for this book were drawn with Derwent coloured pencils
on #502 Canson paper.

Designed by Ron Lightburn
Layout and typography by Kevin Connolly
Photography by See Spot Run
Printed and bound in Canada

Published in Canada by
Doubleday Canada Limited
105 Bond Street, Toronto, Ontario
M5B 1Y3

FRI 10 9 8 7 6 5 4 3 2 1